Do You Know What I'll Do?

Do You Know What I'll Do?

By Charlotte Zolotow

Pictures by Javaka Steptoe

Revised and Newly Illustrated Edition

HarperCollins *Publishers*

One day a little girl said to her little brother . . .

Do you know what I'll do
when the flowers grow again?

I'll pick you a bunch
and you'll be happy.

**Do you know what I'll do
when it snows?**

I'll make you
a snowman.

Do you know what I'll do
when it rains?

I'll catch the rain in a pail
for your plants.

Do you know what I'll do
when the wind blows?

I'll put it in a bottle and let it loose
when the house is hot.

Do you know what I'll do at the seashore?

**I'll bring you a shell
to hold the sound of the sea.**

Do you know what I'll do in the city?

I'll buy you a surprise.

Do you know what I'll do at the movies?

**I'll remember the song
and sing it to you.**

Do you know what I'll do in the night?

**If you have a nightmare,
I'll come and blow on it.**

Do you know what I'll do at the party?

I'll bring you a piece of cake with the candle still in it.

Do you know what I'll do on my walk?

**I'll look at the clouds and
tell you the shapes when I get home.**

Do you know what I'll do
when I wake up?

I'll remember my dreams and
tell them to you.

Do you know what I'll do
when I grow up and have a baby?

I'll bring you my baby to hug. . . .

Like this!

To my sister,
Dorothy Arnof
—C.Z.

Dedicated to the millions of children—but especially in Africa—
who are being ravaged by a disease called AIDS.
What will we do for them?
—J.S.

Do You Know What I'll Do? Text copyright © 2000 by Charlotte Zolotow   Illustrations copyright © 2000 by Javaka Steptoe
Manufactured in China. All rights reserved. http://www.harperchildrens.com

Library of Congress Cataloging-in-Publication Data
Zolotow, Charlotte, 1915–
    Do you know what I'll do? / by Charlotte Zolotow ; pictures by Javaka Steptoe. — Rev. and newly ill. ed.
        p.   cm.
    Summary: A little girl delights her brother with a series of promises about all the wonderful things she'll do to make him
happy as they both grow up.
    ISBN 0-06-027879-X. — ISBN 0-06-027880-3 (lib. bdg.)
    [1. Brothers and sisters—Fiction.   2. Growth—Fiction.]   I. Steptoe, Javaka, 1971–   ill.   II. Title
PZ7.Z77Do   2000   99-26424
[E]—dc21   CIP
                                                                                                          AC

        Typography by Al Cetta   5 6 7 8 9 10   ❖   Revised and newly illustrated edition